This book belongs to

My favourite flower is

For Kevin Littlejohn
and his Dad. SP

For the art club at
Bathford Primary. AB

First published in Great Britain 2004   by Egmont Books Limited

239 Kensington High Street, London W8 6SA

Text copyright © Simon Puttock 2004

Illustrations copyright © Alison Bartlett 2004

A CIP catalogue record for this title is available from The British Library

ISBN 1 4052 0538 5 hb

ISBN 1 4052 0880 5 pb

10 9 8 7 6 5 4 3 2 1

Printed in Italy

Pig's Prize

Simon Puttock
and **Alison Bartlett**

One morning, Pig got a large leaflet through his letter box. It read:

Gardening Competition!

Grow BIG things and win BIG prizes!

"Hurray!" said Pig. "I am good at gardening — I will win EASILY!"

Pig's friends Cow and Dog and Hen all had leaflets, too.
"I shall grow the largest, pinkest water lilies," said Cow.
"In my swimming pool."

"I will grow a great big, creamy cauliflower," said Dog.

"And I will grow wheat," said Hen.
"EXTRA LARGE."

But Pig could not decide WHAT to grow. So he pottered in his greenhouse and had a LONG THINK.

"I know," said Pig. "I will make a special growing mixture, and I'll put a bit on EVERYTHING, and see what grows most."

Pig took a bit of this and a bit of that and some VERY secret ingredients, and he mixed up a lovely, sludgy, smelly mess.

Then Pig went WILD.

He dollopped special growing mixture all over **everything**.

"Now I am bound to win the **biggest** prize," he cried, dancing and rubbing his hands with glee.

Every day, Pig poked and prodded his plants to see if they had grown. The pumpkins were coming along nicely, and so were the cabbage roses. In fact, the whole garden was blooming.

One plant in particular caught Pig's eye.

"That's a fine, big plant," remarked Cow,
one morning. "What sort is it?"
Pig blushed, because he didn't know.
"It's a secret," he said.

By the day of the gardening competition, Pig's mysterious plant was TWICE as tall as Pig, with a bud the size of a football, just about ready to burst.

Cow gave everyone a lift on her tractor.
"Hurry up!" said Hen.
"Come on, Pig," said Dog.
"Beep beep!" Cow tooted the horn.
Pig loaded his plant onto the trailer and off they all drove.

When they got to the gardening competition
they inspected all the other large plants.
Pig was sure that his plant was the biggest.

Soon it was time for the judges to award the prizes.

"Cow," said the judges, "your water lilies are wonderful. You have won a **big** bonnet."

"Dog," said the judges, "your cauliflower is a credit to you. You have won a **big** cookery book."

"Hen," said the judges, "your wheat is very wholesome. You have won a **big** pie dish."

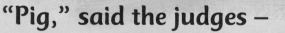

"Pig," said the judges –
"Hurray!" shouted Pig. He was sure he had won the
very best and **biggest** prize of all.

"Pig," said the judges sternly, "do not interrupt. You have grown a **very large weed**. Weeds are not welcome at **this** competition. We are sorry to say that you have won **nothing at all**."

Poor Pig. His great big, beautiful, mysterious plant was only a WEED after all!

When he got home, Pig put his plant back into the garden. He had grown very fond of it.

Then he sat in its leafy shade and felt very sorry for himself.

"Weed," he said, "you are **bigger** and **better** than all the rest. And I don't care what anyone says, **I love you.**"

Just then, Cow and Dog and Hen popped their
heads over the fence.

"Pig," said Cow, "we've been thinking."

"Yes," said Dog, "for a **whole hour**."

"And this is what we thought," said Hen.

"We think your weed is **wonderful**, and you are VERY GOOD at growing things."
Pig perked up a bit. "Yes," he said, "I thought I was."
"So," said Dog. "We want to give you a prize."
Pig perked up a bit more.

It was a great big, creamy cauliflower pie.
It had a golden wheaty crust and a water lily
on top, for decoration.

Pig perked up completely.

"I won!" he cried. "I won the **biggest**, best prize! Hurray for Cow and Hen and Dog, hurray for my weed and **hurray for me!**"

Enjoy more adventures with Pig and his friends in

Pig's Digger

by Simon Puttock
and Alison Bartlett

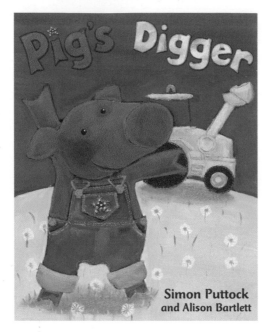

Pig just loves to dig – it's a family thing.
But when Pig gets a **big yellow digger** for his birthday,
he's in danger of going **too far!**

Will Pig and his digger run **riot?**
Or will he come to his senses
with a little help from his friends?

ISBN 1 4052 0231 9

"Hurray!"